THIS CANDLEWICK BOOK BELONGS TO:

_____

_____

_____

_____

Second U.S. paperback edition 1997

Library of Congress Catalog Card Number 95-67994

ISBN 0-7636-0348-1

2 4 6 8 10 9 7 5 3 1

Printed in Hong Kong

This book was typeset in Garamond.
The pictures were done in watercolor and ink.

Candlewick Press
2067 Massachusetts Avenue
Cambridge, Massachusetts 02140

A Bad Start for Santa Claus

Sarah Hayes

illustrated by
Jamie Charteris

CANDLEWICK PRESS
CAMBRIDGE, MASSACHUSETTS

Santa woke up late. He looked
out the window. It was snowing.
It was always snowing.

"It's Christmas Eve today," said Santa.
He jumped out of bed and touched his toes.
Under his bed he could see a toy car.
"Someone might like that," he said, and he
put the car into his spare sack.

He went into the
bathroom to wash his
face and brush his teeth.

When he pulled back
the shower curtain, he
was surprised to find a
large drum.

"My elves are getting
careless," Santa said.
He tapped the drum
with his toothbrush
and dropped the drum
into the sack.

Then he put on his clothes: red underwear,
a long white shirt, a red jacket and hat trimmed with
white fur, and an enormous pair of red pants.

"Now for the boots . . . ," he said. "Maybe I
should get bigger boots next year."

"I need a good breakfast today,"
said Santa. "It's my special day."
He went into the kitchen and
made himself a huge breakfast.

"It's getting late," he said,
and he ate his breakfast
quickly. Someone had left a
teddy bear in the cupboard.
Santa put it into his sack.

Then he remembered something he had forgotten. "My mittens!" he cried. "Where are my mittens? I can't go without them."

He felt in his jacket pockets, but his mittens weren't there. He felt in his front pants pockets, but they weren't there either.

"Oh, dear!" said Santa. "I'll have to search the place, and I'm already late."

He took the elevator down to the workshop.

"Have you seen my mittens?" he asked the elf who ran the elevator.

"No, S.C.," said the elf, "but I did find something in the elevator yesterday." He held out a windup mouse. Santa dropped the mouse into his sack.

In the workshop the elves were busy.

Santa had to shout above the noise.

"I can't find my mittens!" he roared. But the elves were too busy to pay any attention to him. And they were too busy to see a small doll sitting by the elevator.

"You look lost," said Santa, and he gently put the doll into his sack.

The next place to check was the paint shop.
Santa knocked on the door.

The door opened a crack, and a jet of blue
paint shot by him and landed on the wall.

"Sorry, S.C.," said an elf with blue paint on his
hands and face. "What can we do for you?"

"I'm looking for my mittens," said
Santa. "They're red."

"I know that," said the elf.
"They're not here," he added,
"and if they were, they'd be
blue by now." He handed
Santa a bright blue
trumpet and shut
the door.

"Candy factory next," said Santa. It was his favorite place. One of the elves gave him a peppermint stick.

"I'm too full to eat it now," he said. "I'll put it into my sack for safekeeping." Then he hollered above the noise, "Has anyone seen my mittens?"

But no one answered.

Santa was getting worried.

"I might have left my mittens in the packing room," he said. "Maybe they were wrapped up by mistake." When he looked into the packing room, all he could see was a mountain of paper and ribbon and tape.

"Mittens?" he said hopefully. "Red mittens?"

One of the elves emerged from the mountain.

"All mittens are striped this year," he said. "No plain mittens at all. Not plain blue, not plain green, not plain yellow—"

"And not plain red," interrupted Santa. "Oh, no." Then he saw a bag of chocolate coins on the floor. "That doesn't need wrapping," he said, "and it shouldn't be on the floor."

The storeroom had boxes full of presents stacked
up to the ceiling, all neatly labeled. Santa caught
sight of something red behind one of the stacks,
but it was only a yo-yo.

"This doesn't have a label," he said to the elf in charge.

"Oh, take it away," said the elf. "I don't know what to
do with it."

Santa looked at his watch.

"There isn't much time left," he said. "Where could those mittens be?" Then he had an idea. He hurried down the hallway and unbolted the boiler room door.

He turned on the light and walked carefully down the steps.

"No mittens in here," said Santa after searching for a few minutes.

He scrambled up the steps and slipped on a shiny whistle that lay on the top step.

"What a place to leave it," he said.

Now it was time to feed the reindeer.
After the boiler room, the stable felt very cold.
Santa rubbed his hands together to warm them up.
"Where in the world could my mittens be?" he said.
He gave the reindeer an extra large supper.

"Do you know where my mittens are?" he asked.
The reindeer munched their hay and didn't answer.
"Of course you don't," said Santa.
A bright yellow ball lay on top of one of the hay racks.
"We're very sloppy this year," grumbled Santa, and he put
the ball into his sack.

The only place left to look
was the shed where
Santa kept his sleigh.
Two elves were
polishing
the sleigh.

"All ready, S.C.?" they asked.
"Not yet," said Santa. He was starting
to panic. "I can't find my mittens. And if I
can't find my mittens, I can't drive. And if
I can't drive my sleigh, there won't be
any Christmas!"

The elves gasped.
One of them jumped
into the sleigh. "Maybe
they're behind the seat,"
he said. "Here's something."

"What is it? Let me see!" shouted Santa.
The elf held up a painted fan.
"Oh," said Santa. "Oh, no." He
put the fan into his sack and
walked slowly back to the house.
The sack was very
heavy now.

Santa slumped down into an armchair
in the hall. He felt miserable.

"Next year we have to be more organized," he said.
"If there is a next year," he added gloomily.

At that moment a group of elves came running
up to Santa in a panic.

"We're the counters," said one group of elves.

"And we're the checkers," said the other group.

"And we're one sack short!" they all shouted together. "We don't have enough presents to go around."

"And I can't drive the sleigh because I can't find my mittens," said Santa.

"Your mittens are in your back pockets, S.C.,"
said one of the counters. "That's where you
always put them."

Santa stood up. He felt in his
back pocket and found one
red mitten. He felt in his
other back pocket and found
a second red mitten. Santa
smiled a big smile.

"You've solved my problem," he said, "and I think
I can solve yours. Is this what you're looking for?"
　　The elves were amazed. They all spoke at once.
"How did you . . . ? Where on earth . . . ? Where
did you find them?"

"Oh, all over the place," said Santa.
"In the bedroom, in the bathroom,
in the kitchen, in the elevator,

in the workshop, in the paint shop, in the candy factory,
in the packing room, in the storeroom, in the
boiler room, in the stable, in the shed—"

"And in the hall," cried one of the elves, holding up a toy boat he had found under Santa's chair.

"And now," said Santa,

"I really have to leave, or I'll be late.
One minute to go."
  He picked up the sack, put on his big
red mittens, and went outside.

The snow had stopped.

"It's going to be a fine night after all," said
Santa, and he sped off into the darkness.

"Merry Christmas!" shouted the elves, but
Santa Claus was too far away to hear them.